MERMICORN ISLAND #4

Wish upon a Shark

BY JASON JUNE

Scholastic Inc.

Copyright © 2021 by Jason June

Cover and interior art copyright © 2021 by Lisa Manuzak Wiley

All rights reserved. Published by Scholastic Inc., *Publishers since 1920*. SCHOLASTIC and associated logos are trademarks and/or registered trademarks of Scholastic Inc.

The publisher does not have any control over and does not assume any responsibility for author or third-party websites or their content.

ISBN 978-1-338-68521-3

10 9 8 7 6 5 4 3 2 1   21 22 23 24 25

Printed in the U.S.A. 40

First printing 2021

Book design by Yaffa Jaskoll

FEAR-TASTIC FOUR

Brown-and-yellow kelp swished back and forth against my mane. It was so soothing. I had my sketch pad perched on my tail, waiting for **fin-spiration** to strike for my next drawing. Normally, the way the kelp swished helped me concentrate, but not a single idea popped into my head.

"Oh, blobfish," I moaned. "I'm never going to come up with a costume for the Scary Splash Monster Bash."

Scary Splash was my favorite holiday. **Every-fishy** dresses up in creepy costumes, then swims to creatures' doors and screams "Swim-or-sweet!" to get **hoof-fuls** of candy. It's **mer-mazing** and scary in a fun way!

The best part of Scary Splash is the Scary Splash Monster Bash! That's a costume contest where **every-fishy** wears their scariest outfit. Whoever has the creepiest costume gets their very own float in the Scary Splash Parade.

I really wanted to lead the celebration this year.

I'd drawn all kinds of costume ideas like fish skeletons and mermicorn zombies, but nothing felt quite right. I wanted to dress as something that had never been done before.

Just as I lifted my pencil to draw a mummy manatee, a shadow passed over my right shoulder. Tingles ran up and down my tail, and my mane itched like it always does when I'm nervous.

"Hello?" I called.

Another shadow passed on my left. It slithered away through the kelp.

Slithering had to mean it was the electric eels my friend Ruby and I had seen here before. We thought the eels were angry at first, but they were just hungry. I always kept a couple of Ruby's cupcakes that she made with her Baking Sparkle by my side, just in case any of our eel friends needed a treat when I came to draw in the kelp forest.

All mermicorns and sea creatures in Mermicorn Island have magic that we call SPARKLE. Ruby has her BaKing SPARKLE, which lets her make baked goods. Flash has magical superspeed like all seahorses. And because she's a dolphin, Echo has echolocation, which lets her find whatever she's looking for.

My SPARKLE hasn't shown up yet, but I have a treasure chest of magic seashells that hold all kinds of SPARKLE. It was given to me by Poseidon, the most powerful mermicorn in the seven seas.

Maybe there was a magic shell full of SCARY IDEA SPARKLE. I could sure use one, or else I would never win the costume contest at the Scary Splash Monster B–

"BOO!"

"AH!" I screamed. "MONSTER!" I flung my sketch pad down and squeezed my eyes shut. My heart raced and my mane itched all over again as I expected some creepy critter to shriek at me.

But instead of monster roars, I just heard laughter. I peeked an eye open to

find Echo, Flash, and Ruby doubled over
in giggles.

"You practically scared the scales
off my tail," I said. Relief washed over
me that I wasn't about to be eaten by
some mermicorn zombie.

"Sorry," Ruby said through a smile.
"We just couldn't help it."

"Yeah," Flash agreed. "You were so
deep in thought, it was the perfect
opportunity to sneak up on you."

"And get you inspired for the
Monster Bash," Echo added. "How can
you come up with scary ideas if you're
not scared every once in a while?" She
put a flipper out to help me up from
the seafloor. "No hard feelings?"

I took a deep breath to settle my
beating heart. "You got me pretty good."

"Maybe we should change our name
to the **fear-tastic four** instead of

Fin-tastic Four!" Flash said, talking super fast just like he always does. "It's the perfect name for us during Scary Splash."

Flash, Echo, Ruby, and I were BFFFs: best fin friends forever. We called our group of pals the **Fin-tastic Four**. Maybe Flash was right and we could pick a new name for the scary celebration.

"That's a **mer-mazing** idea!" I said. "I can't believe how scared I was. It's like I thought you were the Great Ghost Shark or something."

wait a minnow.

"That's it!" I said. "You **fishies**

scaring me *did* give me **fin-spiration**.

I know what my Monster Bash costume

will be!"

"Ooh, what is it?" Ruby asked. "You

know I always love dressing up!"

I tried to wave my hooves back and

forth as creepily as possible. "The Great

Ghost Shark!"

THE LEGEND OF THE GREAT GHOST SHARK

We swam back to my house while I planned my new Scary Splash Monster Bash costume. As we made our way through town, we passed all kinds of **mer-mazing** monster decorations that **fishies** had hung outside their houses. There were shape-shifting selkie skeletons, moaning mermaids, vampire walruses, and franken-fish! Plus, there were all kinds of oozing brain-o'-lanterns made out of brain coral.

"I can't believe I didn't think of this before," I said. "The legend of the Great Ghost Shark is one of the scariest stories in the seven seas!"

Ruby scrunched her forehead. "How does that one go again?"

I turned my voice into a raspy whisper just like Dad did when he told me this tale on our camping trip last year.

"The story goes that the Great Ghost Shark was the biggest creature in the whole wide ocean," I whispered. "Even bigger than the kraken!"

"What about a magically magnified kraken Sugar Castle?" Flash asked, giggling. "We sure made ours pretty big with that GR⊛W ShelL!"

We couldn't help but laugh. It broke

the scary spell a bit, but then I quickly cleared my throat so I could use my raspy voice again.

"The Great Ghost Shark has teeth the size of sea dragons, and dark red eyes. It would use its magical camouflage to sneak up on whole schools of **fishies** and eat them. Some say that **no-fishy** has seen a kraken in hundreds of years because the Great Ghost Shark"–I took a deep breath and leaped toward Echo–"SWALLOWED THEM WHOLE!"

"Ah!" She jumped back, and her dorsal fin started to shake. "Ooh, that's scary!

My dorsal fin normally shakes from excitement, but this time it's because you gave me the creeps! What ever happened to the Great Ghost Shark anyway?"

"Just like the kraken, **no-fishy** has seen one in thousands of years," I answered. "But my dad said it might not have ever even existed. It's probably just a myth made to send chills up our scales. But either way, I'll be the first Great Ghost Shark **any-fishy** has ever seen, even if it is just in costume."

Flash stretched out his tail. It's what he always does when he's about to use his magical superspeed.

"Could you imagine seeing one of those sharks in real life?" he asked. "I'd take off like this!" He sprinted away and came back in two seconds. "But I promise I'd bring you with me. **NO-fishy's** getting eaten on my watch!"

Ruby laughed. "Good thing the Great Ghost Shark is just a story and we'll never have to worry about seeing a real one in Mermicorn Island."

I stopped floating, and my mouth dropped open.

"You okay, Lucky?" Echo asked. "You

look like you actually *did* see a Great Ghost Shark."

"That's just it," I said. "What if we really did see one? Instead of just making a costume, I could actually turn into a *real* Great Ghost Shark for the

Scary Splash Monster Bash!"

"Silly scales," Flash said. "You're a mermicorn, not a shark. How could you turn into a big mythical beast?"

I was so excited that I practically yelled as loud as I did when my friends scared me: "Poseidon's shells!"

SHAPE-SHIFTING SHOCK

Poseidon's treasure chest sat in its usual spot at the foot of my bed, but this time I had to push my stuffed zombie mermaids off it so I could open the lid. As soon as I did, glittery gold light filled my room. I loved the way the light made my favorite *Manta Lisa* poster shine. The glow also landed on my drawings of Scary Splash monsters that I'd put on my walls. It was so **mer-mazing** (and a little creepy) the way the light made my Dracula dragons' eyes shine!

"So which one is going to get this Great Ghost Shark adventure started?" Echo asked, turning my attention back to the dozens of sparkly shells in the treasure chest.

"Hmm, let me see," I said, and waved my hoof over the pile. I always felt a tug from the tip of my tail to the tip of my horn that pulled me to the shell that would help the most.

This time the tug took my hoof toward an oval-shaped purple shell. Just as I was about to pick it up, it **BALLOONED** so it was perfectly round and changed color to green with orange dots.

"Did you **fishies** see that?" Flash asked. His eyes were as round as the shell. "It changed shape, right? Or are my eyes playing tricks on me?"

Ruby pointed back at the chest. "**Oh my goldfish!** It's doing it again."

She was right. The round shell grew little points and turned bright yellow. It looked a lot like the sun.

"A shell that changes the way it looks has got to have **Shape-Shifting Sparkle**," I said. "Here I go."

I reached forward and grabbed the shell. As soon as I touched it, a warm, tingly, bubbly feeling washed over my scales. That was the feeling of magic!

"Oh, oh, oh, I almost forgot the trident," Flash said. "Be back in a flash." In a **BUBBLE-FILLED BLUR**, Flash was gone and back with his shiny toy trident.

Poseidon let us know that Flash's trident could help me control Shell Sparkle. All I had to do was stick the shell into the base of the trident's prongs, then picture what I wanted the magic to do and wave the trident.

I attached the Shape-Shifting Shell to Flash's toy, but just as I was about to wave it, I realized I didn't know exactly what a Great Ghost Shark looked like.

"I've heard a lot of stories of the big scary shark, but I've never seen a picture," I said. "Maybe we should do some research before I try turning into it."

Echo's dorsal fin shook, this time definitely from excitement. "I bet my dad has some books about it." Echo's dad, Dalton, is an archaeologist. That's a really big word for a **fishy** who studies how other **fishies** used to live in the past.

"But let's still try out the shell to

see if it works," Ruby said. "If I could shape-shift just right, I could try out for any role at the Mermicorn Island Theater!" Other than being a **fin-credible** baker, Ruby is the best actor I know.

"Good idea," I said. "But what shape should I take?"

I floated around my room looking for something to turn into, then realized the perfect **fin-spiration** was already on my walls.

"I could turn into one of these monsters!" I said, pointing at the Scary Splash drawings I'd put up.

My eyes landed on a mummy manatee picture, and I just knew that was the one. I pictured my body bulging out, my skin turning a sickly green, and rotting bandages covering me from mane to tail. Then I waved the trident.

Glitter in all shapes and sizes burst from the Shape-Shifting Shell, which was now rectangular and red with purple stripes. That warm **BUBBLY** magic feeling washed all over my body. Next, my belly got bigger and my tail widened out. Then I felt those oozy gray bandages wrap around my body like a gentle hug.

My friends had their hooves and fins

and flippers over their mouths. They looked **mer-mazed** and disgusted all at the same time.

I drifted in front of my mirror.

"It worked!" I said. "I'm a mummy manatee." I looked totally gross and a bit scary, but in such a **fin-credible** way.

Dad knocked and floated in. When I turned around to say hi, he lost all the color in his face.

"M-m-m-m-m-m-m–," Dad stuttered. He couldn't get any words out. He was so scared, he had to use his BUbbLe SPaRKLe to spell the word **MUMMY** in **BUBBLES** that burst from his horn.

"Dad, it's okay. It's just me!" I said. "I'm so sorry. I didn't mean to scare you."

But it was too late. He sped out of the room, calling for my mom to find me and get out of the house.

I looked to my friends, and we all laughed.

"I guess that means the Shape-Shifting Shell Sparkle totally works," I said. "But before we plan out the Great Ghost Shark costume, I'd better change back and find Dad."

FOUR IS BETTER
THAN ONE

It didn't take long to calm Dad down once

I changed back. When I told him and

Mom that the **Shape-Shifting Shell**

let me turn into a mummy manatee, Dad

laughed and Mom said, "With magic that

good, you're bound to win the Scary

Splash Monster Bash tomorrow!"

"I'll transform into the scariest monster of all," I told them. "I'm going to be the Great Ghost Shark!"

BUBBLES burst out of Dad's horn to spell **AAAH! SCARY!** But he was smiling so I knew he thought it was a good idea.

"And what are you **fishies** going to be?" Mom asked Ruby, Echo, and Flash.

My friends looked at one another and shrugged. Guilt guppies swam in my stomach. I'd talked so much about my costume that I hadn't offered to help my friends come up with theirs.

"Oh, blobfish!" I moaned. "I'm

sorry, **every-fishy**. I got so caught up in the Great Ghost Shark and put all the attention on me. We should try to win the costume contest as a team so we can all lead the Scary Splash Parade together."

wait a minnow. An idea swam into my head.

"What's scarier than one Great Ghost Shark?" I asked.

Flash raised his fin. "Ooh, ooh, ooh. I know this one! A *hungry* Great Ghost Shark!" His stomach rumbled. "Speaking of which, can we have some snacks?"

I laughed. "That would be scary, but

I was thinking *four* Great Ghost Sharks. Why don't we go as a whole school of the scary monsters?"

"Can you imagine four of those beasts swimming into the Mermicorn Island Theater at once?" Ruby asked with wide eyes. "It'll be my most dramatic performance yet. I'm in!"

"Me too!" said Echo. "This will be the creepiest adventure of my life."

"And with me that makes us the **Fear-tastic Four**!" Flash said. "This is going to rock! No, wait. This is going to *shock!*"

"**Mer-mazing!**" I cheered. "Let's

get to work. We've only got one day to get everything ready for the Monster Bash."

With that, we put together the plan for the creepiest costumes Mermicorn Island would ever see.

First, we went to Echo's house to

read through her dad's books and see
what we could find about the Great
Ghost Shark. One even had pictures
that were so fearsome we all jumped.
In the book's illustrations, the Great
Ghost Shark was super pale and bigger
than a blue whale, and had the reddest
eyes I'd ever seen. After our GR☻W
Shell mishap, we decided we could
still be scary sharks, but we'd stay
normal-sized so we didn't cause another
massive mess.

Next, I drew a design of the four of
us as sharks, and we thought of ideas
to make ourselves look even creepier.

Ghost Shark

Blue Whale

We decided we could cover our fins
in rotten seaweed, and we could wear
necklaces of broken shell bits to make
it look like we had even more gruesome
teeth and to be extra scary. Echo used
her echolocation to find the materials,
and Flash sped around town in a magical

superspeed second to gather them.

Ruby kept our stomachs from growling like monsters by making shark-shaped cinnamon rolls. They were **sea-licious**, and she even made their eyes red with sea cherries!

By the end of the day, all was set to become the **fear-tastic four** Great Ghost Sharks!

SCARY SPLASH
MONSTER BASH

The next day, Echo, Flash, Ruby, and I floated backstage at the Mermicorn Island Theater, where **every-fishy** in the Monster Bash costume contest was lining up. Our parents all sat in the crowd, ready to be wowed and creeped out by our Great Ghost Shark transformation.

Based on the funny looks we were getting from other creatures in the contest, they were ready for our outfits too. **Fishies** kept asking where our costumes were, since we looked like our normal selves.

Echo's dorsal fin shook. "They're going to be so **mer-mazed** when we

shape-shift onstage," she whispered excitedly.

"It's going to be so dramatic!" Ruby added.

Our plan was to wait until we got onstage. Then Flash would use a burst of superspeed to get our rotten seaweed and broken shell teeth right when I waved the Shape-Shifting Shell to turn us all into Great Ghost Sharks.

"We're going to make the scariest splash at the Monster Bash!" I said.

Mayor Vanderhoof swam to the stage, which was covered in coral brain-o'-lanterns, and clapped her hooves together.

"**Mer-monsters** and **Franken-fish**, can I have your attention, please?" she called. "It's time for the Scary Splash Monster Bash!"

Every-fishy in the audience cheered and whistled.

"As you know, the costume contest kicks off the Monster Bash every year," the mayor explained. "Whoever we vote as the scariest costume gets to lead the Scary Splash Parade. Now, who's ready to be scared?"

My friends and I hollered along with

the audience as the first contestant took the stage. But as every new creature came up in their costume, my cheers got quieter as my confidence got smaller. The costumes were good. Scary good.

Roger the jellyfish dressed as a zombie and used his stinging tentacles to shock a bunch of creepy zombie dolls so they jumped and jolted across the stage. A mermicorn with CAMOUFLAGE SPARKLE would disappear and jump out at different sea creatures in the audience. A group of selkies used their own Shape-Shifting magic and

turned into hairy, snarling **were-whales** with claws on their flippers.

Each new costume was scarier and more fun than the last. And I couldn't help but notice that each contestant used their own SPARKLE to make

their costume extra creepy. If I
didn't have Poseidon's magic shells,
I wouldn't have stood a chance against
their outfits.

"Lucky," Flash whispered, nudging my
shoulder. "It's time for us to go on. You
ready?"

He handed me his trident, complete
with the Shape-Shifting Shell in it.
The shell must have known it was Scary
Splash because it was now in the shape
of a sea dragon skull.

I grabbed the trident and took a
deep breath. It was okay if I didn't
have magic of my own. I had my shells,

and no matter what, I had the **Fin-tastic Four** to help me through anything.

"Let's do this!" I said, and we all floated onstage. Our parents cheered the loudest when the spotlight hit the four of us.

"Get ready to have the scare of your lives," Ruby called, which was my cue to raise the trident. When I had it straight up in the air, Flash left and came back in two seconds. He draped the rotten seaweed and broken shell teeth he'd grabbed around our necks.

I pictured the four of us turning

into pale sharks with bright red eyes,
then waved the trident over me and my
friends.

Sparkles of every color flew from
the Shape-Shifting Shell, and I
felt those warm magic tingles run from
my tail to my mane. I turned to my

friends to see them shift into Great Ghost Sharks right before my eyes.

Ruby opened her new sharp teeth-filled shark mouth to yell, "Behold the Great Ghost Sharks!"

AND THE CROWD GOES WILD

For a minnow, no-fishy said anything. Their mouths all dropped open as they took in the four Great Ghost Sharks in front of them. Then it was like they all took a breath together and started cheering and clapping and laughing and hollering.

"So scary!"

"That's brilliant!"

"I thought I'd never see a Great Ghost Shark ever in my life!"

I turned to my friends. They definitely looked a lot scarier than normal!

Flash's sharp teeth turned up into a huge grin. "This is **mer-mazing**! **Every-fishy** will remember our costume for years. Maybe *we'll* even become legends like the Great Ghost Shark!"

Ruby pulled us into a huddle. "The show doesn't have to be over yet," she said. "Let's be extra scary. On the count of three, let's all roar at the same time."

Even as a shark, Echo's dorsal fin shook. "This is going to be **fin-credible**."

We floated into position. Then Ruby held up a ghostly white flipper and counted: "One, two, three."

We each let loose a fearsome roar. With the four of us together, it made the walls of the Mermicorn Island Theater shake.

Fishies' eyes went wide all across the room. Some even covered their ears.

One mermaid hid under her chair, but she was laughing so I knew it was all in good fun.

The mayor swam back onstage, grinning from ear to ear. She turned to the crowd and said, "I think we can all agree that these four are our Scary Splash Monster Bash winners."

The whole room burst into applause. I couldn't believe we'd won. The Shape-Shifting Shell worked!

"Well, then, let's get the parade party started!" Mayor Vanderhoof said, and she led the crowd out into Mermicorn Island Square, where all types of **mer-mazingly** creepy floats waited. One looked like the Loch Ness Monster, another was full of ice beasts made by sea dragons, and a third was shaped like the Boogie Barracuda, who hides under your bed.

Ruby, Echo, Flash, and I were still in our shark forms and swam to the float at the very front of the line. It was the Loch Ness Monster float. Humans think Nessie is scary, but **every-fishy** knows he's just a friendly guy

who vacations in Mermicorn Island sometimes.

While we were about to climb into the float, I noticed a dark shadow in the distance heading toward the square.

"Is there another float coming for the parade, Mayor Vanderhoof?" I asked.

She looked at the shadow with a big scowl on her face. "That's strange. All the floats should have checked in before the costume contest."

"It's moving pretty fast," Flash said. "I should know. I am superspeedy, after all."

"But what is it?" Echo asked, then let loose a few of her magical echolocation clicks, which help her see things far away. "Um, **every-fishy**. That critter looks like *us*."

Ruby turned toward Echo. "You mean it looks like us in our costumes?"

Echo slowly nodded.

"That means it's a—"

"GREAT GHOST SHARK!" **Fishies** everywhere screamed and pointed above the square as the dark shadow became crystal clear.

It really was a Great Ghost Shark. But it wasn't small like me and my friends. It was *gigantic*! Its ghostly pale skin was even paler than ours, and its red eyes were redder than I could have imagined. But there was one thing about it that stood out the most:

It had tons and tons of sharp teeth. Teeth that were opening.

And coming right toward us.

SCARED IN THE SQUARE

The Great Ghost Shark hovered over Mermicorn Island Square. It was way bigger than when Nelia was magically magnified by the GROW Shell. When I looked up, all I could see was the shark's ghostly pale skin and red eyes.

Every-fishy started swimming away in a panic. Mom and Dad and

my friends' parents raced toward us.
Flash's parents got there first with their
superspeed, just as the Great Ghost
Shark opened its way-too-big mouth.

"Oh my goldfish," Ruby said as
row after row of sharp teeth revealed
itself.

"What do we do?" Echo asked.

"We're going to get you out of here," Flash's mom said, holding out her fins. "Grab on and I'll—"

"Help! Where am I?"

We all looked up. The Great Ghost Shark wasn't opening their mouth to eat us. They were talking.

"Please, help me," they said again. "My name is Doris, and I don't know how I got here. Where are my parents?"

Flash's eyes went wide. "You're a kid? Just like us? Why are you so big?"

Instead of looking fearsome and scary, Doris now looked confused and worried. "I was going to ask why you

four are so small. I heard your roar
and followed it, thinking you might be my
parents. You are Great Ghost Sharks,
aren't you?"

"Not exactly," I said. I waved the
trident with the now heart-shaped
Shape-Shifting Shell. With a rush of
warm tingles, we turned back into our
normal selves. "We used magic to look
like Great Ghost Sharks for the Scary
Splash Monster Bash."

Gigantic tears formed in Doris's eyes.
"Oh no," she whimpered. "I'm never going
to find them."

The rest of our parents had finally

made it back to us. I instantly felt safe, just like I always did when Mom and Dad were around. Poor Doris must be really scared without hers.

"I've got a SHRiNK SHell back home that can get you to a size so you can stay safe with us," I yelled up to Doris. "Then we can look for your parents. How does that sound?"

Doris wiped her tears away with her massive pale fins. "That sounds okay."

I turned to Flash. "Can you take me to my treasure chest?" I asked. "That way we can be there and back in a flash."

"You know I'm always happy to help. Let's go!" Flash took my fin, and in no time, I was back in my bedroom. I found the tiny pink ShRINK ShELL I'd used to shrink Nelia back to her normal size. Then we burst back into the square, where I swam up to Doris.

Before meeting her, I would have been afraid to be so close to razor-sharp teeth that were twice as big as me. But I could see in her face how sad and scared she was to be without her parents, and knew we had to help.

"I'm going to use this ShELL SPARKLE, and you'll feel some warm magic

BUBBLES," I said. "Then you'll be small enough to fit inside the square. Ready?"

Doris nodded. I pictured her being the same size as me and my friends, then waved the trident. Bright pink glitter burst over Doris, and she shrunk right

before my eyes. She was so big that it took longer than I expected.

When she was finally my size, I pointed down to the square. "Come on," I said. "Let's go find your parents."

PARENT PURSUIT

The first thing I did was bring Doris over to my friends. They sure know how to make me feel better whenever I'm upset.

"I'm so sorry you're lost," Ruby said. "Is it okay if I hug you?"

Doris gave a weak smile. "Thank you, but I'd rather not. I just want to find my mom and dad."

Ruby nodded and said, "We'll find them. I promise."

"Yeah," Echo agreed. "Let's see if they're anywhere nearby. Come on, Dads!" She grabbed her dads' flippers. "Let's use our echolocation and see what comes up." Echo and her parents swam away, letting loose their magical clicks and whistles that could help them locate anything, as long as it wasn't too far away.

"Hey, we can help too!" Flash said, stretching between Mr. and Mrs. Finnegan. "We'll use our superspeed around town and see if

any Great Ghost Sharks are floating nearby. Ready, Mom? Ready, Dad?"

"Be back soon!" Flash's mom said, and they were gone in a burst of **BUBBLES**.

My mom drifted forward and asked, "Where did you last see your parents, Doris?"

Doris chewed on her cheek while she thought. "Last night. I went to sleep at my grandparents' house in the Mariana Trench, but sometimes I sleep-swim. I woke up and was completely lost. Then I heard the Great Ghost Shark roar, and thought it might be my parents."

Guilt guppies swam in my stomach. "That was us in our monster costumes. We roared for the crowd, and you must have heard it."

"Why would you dress up as a Great Ghost Shark for a monster?" Now Doris looked hurt as well as scared that she'd lost her parents. Even more guilt guppies dashed through my belly.

"I'm sorry," I said. "You seem really nice. I can see now that all those legends of Great Ghost Sharks swallowing towns whole are completely wrong."

Doris stuck out her tongue. "Ew, yuck! We don't eat *towns*. Speaking of which"—Doris rubbed her belly—"I am really hungry."

Ruby perked up. "That's something I can help with. Do you like cake?"

Doris looked happy for the first time since she'd floated into Mermicorn Island. "I love it! Kelp Kreme Cake is my favorite."

"Coming right up!" Ruby squinted her eyes and wiggled her tail. Then, in a burst of red glitter, a beautiful Kelp Kreme Cake appeared.

Ruby handed it to Doris. "There's more where that came from if you're still hungry."

Doris took the cake and gobbled it down. **"sea-licious!"**

I looked around while **every-fishy** who was scared before crowded back in to the square. Most were still in their creepy costumes, but they weren't focused on having a Scary Splash Parade anymore. Now they were trying to help Doris find her parents.

The sea dragons shot bursting iceworks, hoping any passing Great Ghost Shark would see their bright colors. The mermaids used their magical singing to try to lure Doris's parents to the square. Plus, all the dolphins and seahorses joined Echo and Flash in their search. Ruby and Baxter Beluga kept **every-fishy** fed with baked treats.

Meanwhile, I just floated there. I didn't have any magic that could help.

"wait a minnow," I said. "Maybe there's some kind of ShaRk Shell SPaRkle in Poseidon's chest." I turned to my parents. "Is it okay if I run home really quick? I want to find a magic shell that could help."

"Of course," Dad said. "We'll go with you."

"Can I go too?" Doris asked. "All

these scary decorations are kind of freaking me out."

It was funny to think that something I used to think was a monster could get just as frightened as **every-fishy** else during Scary Splash.

"Absolutely," I said.

We were off to see if I could lend a **helping hoof**.

GREAT GHOST SHARK
SECRET

Usually it took me a long time to swim
home while I looked at all the Scary
Splash decorations on **every-fishy's**
house, but that day I swam almost as
fast as Flash. I had to find some way to
help Doris get to her parents.

As soon as we swam through the

front door, Doris and I burst into my room and opened up Poseidon's chest of magic shells.

"Those shells are **sea-utiful**," Doris said.

She was right. The shells glittered and sparkled just like they always did, but something was off.

I didn't feel a tug in my hooves. Or in my tail. Not a single scale buzzed with that magical feeling that pulled me toward the shell with the right type of SPARKLE to help.

"How do they work?" Doris asked. She reached forward and picked up the very first shell I had ever used: the spiral blue INVISIBILITY Shell. Doris disappeared right before my eyes.

"Oh my goldfish," she cried. "I'm invisible!" She reappeared soon after when she gently put the shell back in the treasure chest. "That's definitely not the shell I need right now. My parents will never find me if they can't see me. Which shell do you think will help?"

My heart sank into the tip of my tail. "Well, normally I feel a pull toward the one that should have the right magic. But…I don't feel anything. I'm so sorry, Doris. Poseidon said sometimes magic can't solve our problems, and I guess this might be one of those times."

Suddenly, my window flew open and Flash sped inside. Ruby and Echo were with him too. They each held on to one of his fins.

"What'd we miss?" Flash asked. "Did you find a shell that could get us to Doris's parents?"

I shook my head. "No. It's the first time that I've never felt a pull toward the shells." I didn't think it was possible, but it felt like my heart sank even further. "What if I can't make the shells work anymore? What if I don't even have **Shell Sparkle**?"

Ruby swam forward and gave me a hug. "It's okay if you don't," she said. "**Every-fishy** is helping."

"That's right," Echo agreed. "With seahorse superspeed, dolphin

echolocation, and every mermicorn using their SPARKLE, we are for sure going to find those Great Ghost Sharks."

"Okay," I said, but my heart wasn't in it. I definitely wanted to find Doris's mom and dad, but I wished that I could help. Somehow I was the only creature in all of Mermicorn Island who couldn't use magic to help in the Great Ghost Shark Search.

That's when it clicked. I wasn't the only one not using special powers.

"Doris," I said, turning to my new ghostly friend. "**Every-fishy** in Mermicorn Island has magic. Do Great Ghost Sharks have magic too?"

Doris looked nervously at the floor. "Yes, but..." She paused. "My parents told me never to share it."

"Oh, well, I wouldn't want you to get in trouble," I said. "I just thought it might be able to help with the search."

Doris chewed on her cheek again, which surprisingly didn't seem to hurt even though her teeth were extra jagged. She looked like she was bursting to tell us something.

"Are you okay, Doris?" Flash asked. "When I fidget around like that, it's because I have to use the bathroom. I can show you where the toilet is."

"No, it's not that," Doris said. "I think maybe my magic can help. But if I tell you what it is, you promise not to share it with **any-fishy** else?"

"We promise," my friends and I all said at the same time. Then we busted

up in giggles. But even though we were laughing, Doris still looked anxious.

"Okay, here it goes," she said, and took a deep breath. She even looked over her shoulder like she thought other **fishies** might be eavesdropping. When

she saw that the coast was clear, Doris
finally told us what type of SPARKLE
she had.

"Great Ghost Sharks can grant
wishes."

YOUR WISH IS MY COMMAND

Our mouths hung open so wide that a regular-sized Great Ghost Shark could have swum in them.

Finally, Flash ended our **mer-mazed** silence. "You mean like a Wish-upon-a-Starfish?" he asked. "We saw a whole Sugar Castle made out of those once. And a doughnut too. The Blue sisters ate it and wished for more, then *ta-da!* Another doughnut appeared!"

"Not quite like that," Doris said. "Wish-upon-a-Starfish can only grant small wishes."

"Like wishing for another doughnut," Echo said.

Doris nodded. "Yes, magically small things like wishing for more food or for something to change color are what Wish-upon-a-Starfish are for. But Great Ghost Sharks have much more power. It's why we're so big. Our bodies need to be large enough to hold all that strong magic."

Ruby's eyes popped open. "I just had the best idea! All you have to do is wish for your parents to find you."

Doris's sharp teeth drooped into a frown. "I wish it were that easy. Great

Ghost Sharks can't make wishes for themselves. They can only grant wishes for others."

"So if **any-fishy** swims up to you and makes a wish, your magic can make it happen?" I asked.

Doris looked nervous again, but she slowly nodded. "That's why Great Ghost Sharks went into hiding all those years ago. With the power to grant any wish imaginable, so many **fishies** thought that they could use our WISH SPARKLE whenever they wanted. They were using us for our powers instead of connecting with us through our hearts.

So we made up scary stories about ourselves and went away."

My whole life I thought it would be so great to have SPARKLE of my own. I never thought that magic could end up seeming like a curse.

"But please, please don't tell **any-fishy**," Doris said again. "It's why my parents made me promise not to tell."

I floated close to Doris and crossed a hoof over my chest. "Cross my heart," I said. "But I am going to ask you to use your WiSh SPARKLE. Just once."

Doris's eyes got wide, and she seemed really scared. She looked like we all did when she first swam into town.

"Please don't," Doris whispered.

"It's going to be okay," I said. "Because, Doris, I wish that your parents would find you."

Gold glitter burst out of Doris's jagged teeth. It danced and swirled around Doris until it gathered together in a big gold ball and zoomed out my bedroom window. Then everything went silent.

"**Oh, blobfish,**" I moaned. "I guess it didn't work."

Doris's eyes filled with tears, Flash slunk to the floor, Ruby let out a huge sigh, and Echo pounded her flipper against my desk. We were all so disappointed. Not only did I not have my own magic, I couldn't even help **some-fishy** else use their SPARKLE.

I drifted to my door. "I guess we could see if my parents know what to d– Oh!"

The floor started shaking. My bed and desk and mirror bounced, making so much noise. The walls shook so much that my *Manta Lisa* poster fell and my jellyfish lamp crashed to the floor.

Then an earsplitting roar boomed all around us. It was the most fearsome sound I had ever heard.

Maybe it was because of all the Scary Splash stuff around town, but I couldn't stop the scream that jumped from my mouth.

"MONSTER!"

While Echo, Flash, Ruby, and I shook like **scaredy-fish**, Doris swam to my window and looked up. Her frown turned into the biggest smile.

"That's not a monster, silly," Doris said. "That's my mom and dad!"

"wait a minnow," I said. "Your **SPARKLE** worked?"

Doris nodded and swam out of my

bedroom. "Come on," she called. "I'll introduce you."

We raced out of the house and into my front yard. It was surprisingly dark. All the light from above was blocked out by two humongous creatures. Floating side by side, they covered the entire town! It would have been scary, but when I gazed up, I saw the most **sea-utiful** creatures in the whole wide ocean.

MEET THE PARENTS

They were sharks. Totally gigantic,
super huge sharks. Only their skin was
rainbow-colored, and their hundreds
of teeth were shaped like hearts. Their
eyes also had a **fin-credible** gold glow
that made me really calm.

"**Every-fishy**," Doris said,
pointing up at the two creatures,

"meet my mom, Iris, and my dad, Thad."

"You're grown-up Great Ghost Sharks?" Flash asked. "You don't look like ghosts at all!"

Doris laughed. "We grow out of our sharp teeth and gray skin when we get older." Doris flashed a big, sharp-toothed grin and pointed at her mouth. "These are just my baby teeth."

Iris scooped her daughter up in a huge fin, then held her right in front of one of her big golden eyes. "Oh, honey, we've been worried sick." She smooshed her gently against her cheek.

"You're so small," Thad said. "What happened?"

Doris swam back down to float next to me and my friends. "Mom, Dad, these are my new friends: Lucky, Ruby, Echo, and Flash. When I sleep-swam away, I floated into this town. Lucky used **ShRink SPaRkle** to make sure I could stay safely with them while we tried to find you. Then we used my—" Doris stopped herself and slapped her fins over her mouth.

"Doris," Thad said, and looked at her suspiciously. "What did you do?"

"We, um... we used my WISH SPARKLE," Doris whispered.

Iris turned so her ear hole was leaning toward us. "A little louder, sweetheart. We're way up here, you know."

Doris cleared her throat. I could tell she was really nervous.

"We used my WISH SPARKLE," she said. "I told Lucky about my magic, and he wished for you to find me. I know I promised I would never ever tell about our secret **Sparkle**, but it was an emergency."

Both of Doris's parents turned their golden eyes toward me. They were **sea-utiful**, but it still made me a little scared to have two huge critters staring at me.

"Please don't be mad at Doris," I said. "I asked her to tell us about your magic because I thought it could help. And it did, so everything worked out great, right?"

Iris and Thad both reached a fin down and picked me up, lifting me closer and closer to their mouths. Even though their teeth were heart-shaped, they were still teeth. And her parents could still swallow me whole.

"Please don't eat me!" I shrieked.

Thad laughed. It was so deep it sent ripples through the water. Iris laughed too, and it sounded like chimes.

"Eat you?" Thad chuckled. "We would never."

"That's right," Iris said with a wink. "You'd be much too chewy. We just wanted to thank you for reuniting our family."

I was floating so high above my friends and parents that they all looked like little shrimp. "My family and the **Fin-tastic Four** mean the whole ocean to me," I said. "So I knew I had

to help Doris find you. I was worried that I wouldn't be able to, since none of my magic shells helped and I don't have any SPARKLE of my own like **every-fishy** else."

Iris's big mouth popped into an O shape. "Lucky, I have something I need

to talk with my husband about for **just a minnow**."

She gently lowered me back down to the seafloor. I had been so high up, it felt like it took forever.

We all looked up as Doris's parents whispered together. It sounded like the *swish swish swish* of water when there's a thunderstorm above the surface.

"What are they talking about?" I asked.

Doris shook her head. "I have no idea."

"Sometimes parents just need time to talk," Dad explained. "Everything will be A-okay."

Finally, Doris's parents turned to us. They were both smiling, and the rainbow colors on their skin shined brighter.

"Lucky," Thad said, "we'd like to give you a gift."

"For finding our daughter," Iris added, "and wishing us together."

I felt excited bubbles in my belly.

"Really, you don't have to do that. I know if I couldn't find my family or friends, I'd be so scared. And not the fun kind of scared like during Scary Splash."

Iris smiled at me. "It's that sense of selflessness that we want to reward," she said. "You mentioned that your own SPARKLE hasn't developed yet. Would you like it to, Lucky?"

Tingles ran from my tail to my horn. "More than anything in the whole wide ocean!" I loved having Poseidon's chest full of magic shells, but when none of them could help in the Great Ghost Shark Search, I felt like a real **blobfish** that I didn't have magic of my own.

"Can you do that?" Flash asked. "Give Lucky SParKle, I mean? Your magic must be really, really strong if it can make SParKle."

Thad nodded. "Our magic has the ability to grant any wish, no matter how big. Since you used Doris's WISh SParKle for good rather than selfish reasons, we'd like to do this for you."

"Think of all the new adventures we could have," Echo said.

Ruby smiled. "And no matter what you choose, we'll always be the Fin-tastic Four."

"The choice is yours, Lucky," Iris said. "All you have to do is make a wish."

MAKE A WISH

on my goldfish. All that I had ever hoped for was being offered by the most magical sharks I'd ever heard of.

I looked at my mom and dad. "Can I?" I asked.

Mom and Dad looked at each other, then turned to me and nodded.

"The choice is up to you," Dad said.

"If you want your own SParkle, wish away."

Mom swam forward and wrapped me in a hug. "Just know we love you exactly as you are. Whether your own SParkle shows up years from now, whether you

wish for it from the Great Ghost Sharks, or even if your SPARKLE never comes. You've brought so much love into our lives, Lucky. That's the greatest magic of all."

Mom's eyes filled with tears, but I could tell they were the happy kind.

I thought about what she said. What if my own SPARKLE never showed up? I knew I'd still have my friends and my parents, but I'd always dreamed of having magic of my own.

"I think I'd like that," I said.

Iris flashed a big toothy smile. "Just say the words, sweetheart."

I took a deep breath. All the

memories of me and the **Fin-tastic Four** using the magic shells swam through my head. My heart filled with hope picturing all the new adventures Echo mentioned we could have.

I knew what I wanted to do.

"I wish I had my own **SParkle**," I said.

Doris's parents' eyes glowed an even brighter gold. The rainbow stripes on their bodies pulsed. Then glitter of every color burst from their heart-shaped teeth and showered over me.

That magic feeling I'd always felt of warm tingly **BUBBLES** washed along my mane and horn and scales, but this time it was so much stronger. It felt so good it made me laugh.

My friends and family laughed along too. Their eyes were so wide watching me that I could see the Ghost Sharks' multicolored SPARKLE reflected in them.

Just as soon as it started, everything stopped. The glitter fizzed away, and I floated there looking just like I had before.

"How do you feel?" Ruby asked.

"Yeah," Flash said. "What kind of magic is in you? Show us, show us, show us!"

To be honest, I didn't feel different.

Maybe even the Great Ghost Sharks'
WISH SPARKLE couldn't give me magic.

"I don't know how," I said. "I've only
ever used the shells."

Echo's dorsal fin shook. "Ooh! Maybe
you could try finding something. Just
picture in your mind what you want to

find, and if you have FINDING SPARKLE,
it'll show you where it is."

The first thing that popped into my
mind was Flash's toy trident we used
to control SHELL SPARKLE. As soon as it
appeared in my head, purple glitter burst
from my horn and formed itself into an
arrow pointing toward Flash's house.

"It worked!" I shouted.

"Congratulations, Lucky," Doris said.
"Now you have your own magic!"

"That's **fin-credible**," Flash cried.
"Although I was kind of hoping you'd
have SUPERSPEED SPARKLE."

"That would have been neat," I said,

and thought about what it would be like
to swim in a magical sprint alongside Flash.

"Wait a minnow," I whispered.
While I thought about sprinting with
Flash, the scales on my tail started to
tingle. Then they glowed orange. I felt
this huge urge to swim, so I did. And
I was fast!

"Holy mackerel!" I cheered. The
street rushed by in a blur, all kinds of
Scary Splash decorations swinging in my
wake. I circled back to my house and
stopped right in front of my friends. I
wasn't even out of breath.

"No way!" Flash said. "You *do*

have **SUPERSPEED SPARKLE**. And
FINDING SPARKLE too! I've never
heard of **any-fishy** having multiple
kinds of magic before." Flash sped
forward and gave me a **high fin**.

Ruby tapped a hoof against her
chin. "Hang on. There is one mermicorn

we know who can do every type of SPARKLE known to **merkind**. Maybe you can too! Just like Poseidon! Try making a cupcake."

I pictured a wriggly electric eel cupcake like Ruby had made for Flash's birthday party. Then I squinted my eyes shut, wiggled my tail, and red glitter burst from my horn. It turned into an eel cupcake before our eyes.

"It worked!" I said, then looked up at Doris's parents. "You gave me all the magic in the ocean?"

Iris shook her head. "We didn't give it to you. It was already inside you, just waiting to be unleashed."

"It's called Seven Seas Sparkle," Thad added. "That's the magic that lets you control every type of Sparkle. As your brilliant friend Ruby noted, it is the same power Poseidon has."

"Whooooa," I breathed. "Every type of Sparkle?"

"Yes," Iris said. "You'll need to practice so that your Sparkle can get stronger, but when you grow up, you could be as strong as Poseidon."

"That's a lot of power, Lucky," Mom said. "Which takes a lot of responsibility. Do you think you're up for it?"

I looked over at Doris, who couldn't stop smiling since we found her parents. I knew that as long as I had Seven Seas Sparkle, I wanted to use it to help **every-fishy** I could.

"I am, Mom," I said. "I promise to always use my magic to lend a **helping hoof**. Like this."

I pictured Doris back in her normal size. Huge orange bubbles burst from my horn and wriggled over her. She pulled and stretched and grew until she was floating over us as her big Great Ghost Shark self. But there was one very noticeable change.

"Oh!" Doris said with wide eyes. "My rainbow skin just appeared!"

"You're growing up so fast," Thad said.

"Goodbye, Lucky," Doris said with a wave. "Thank you for all your help. I'll never forget you."

"Thank *you*," I called back. "If it wasn't for you and your parents, I wouldn't have my SPARKLE."

"That's not exactly true," Ruby said.

"Yeah," Flash added. "You're the one who brought us all together."

"Trust us," Echo said. "You had your own special SPARKLE all along."

POSEIDON PARADE
POINTERS

Doris and her parents waved goodbye
and left Mermicorn Island in a **sea-
utiful** rainbow blur. They had to get
back to Doris's grandparents' place for
their own Scary Splash celebrations.

"**Oh my goldfish**, Scary Splash!"
Echo cried as the Great Ghost Sharks

swam away. "Do you think the parade is still on?"

"There's only one way to find out," I said, and held out my hooves for Ruby and Echo to take. "We'll race you, Flash!"

Using my **Seven Seas Sparkle**, I pictured magical superspeed getting us to Mermicorn Island Square in the blink of an eye. And just like that, it happened!

But Flash still got there first. "I'm going to need to practice so one day I'll win!" I told him.

The square was steadily filling with **fishies** again. They were still in their costumes, and the Scary Splash floats

were still lined up, ready for the parade

to begin.

"Well done, fearless **fishies**,"

Mayor Vanderhoof said as she swam

through the crowd. "Reuniting Doris with

her parents *and* having the scariest

costumes around. It's been a big night for the four of you."

Ruby looked at her watch. "I know it's later than usual, but are we still able to have the parade?"

Flash's stomach rumbled. "Yeah, saving Great Ghost Sharks really worked up an appetite. I need some parade candy!"

The mayor laughed and motioned toward the Loch Ness Monster float at the front of the line. "Hop in your float and we'll get started. Oh, by the way, a special guest is waiting for you."

We all turned to look at the float. Sitting in the front seat was a mermicorn who looked very familiar, with a gigantic gold trident resting next to him.

"Whoa!" I said as we swam up to him. "That's the best Poseidon costume I've ever seen."

"Costume!" the mermicorn said in the most booming voice. "It's me! Poseidon!"

Flash raised his fin in the air. "Ooh, ooh, ooh! Do you remember me, Mr. Poseidon, sir? We met in Atlantis earlier this year."

Poseidon laughed. "Of course I remember you, Flash. I'm here today to congratulate Lucky on getting his Seven Seas Sparkle."

Poseidon placed his hoof on my shoulder. "I knew all along that type of magic would come to you, Lucky."

"You did?" I asked. "Does that mean we have FORTUNE-TELLER SPARKLE in us too?"

Poseidon nodded. "It does, and every other type of SPARKLE you can think of. It is a lot of pressure to have all that magic at your hooftips. I gave you those magic shells so you could understand the joys and mishaps that can come with access to so much power. You've handled it very well, and I'm so proud of you."

"What do I do now?" I asked.

"That's up to you," Poseidon said. "Now that you have your SEVEN SEAS SPARKLE, I'll be taking back the shells. But if you always remember to share the magic that's inside you, I know you'll make the ocean a better place."

Never in a million years did I think I'd someday have all the magic in the seven seas. Not too long ago I was sad that I was the only mermicorn at school without any SPARKLE. I guess sometimes you just have to wait and see how everything works out.

"I promise to always share the magic," I said. "And I know just how to start."

I pictured me and my friends back in our Great Ghost Shark costumes. Multicolored glitter burst from my horn, and in no time at all the four of us transformed. Only this time we looked like Doris with her rainbow-colored skin.

"Let's get this parade started," I yelled, and the whole square burst into applause.

Echo, Flash, Ruby, and I piled into the float with Poseidon by our side. We drifted through the town, laughing and looking at Scary Splash decorations and gobbling up candy. I knew no matter what kind of powers came to me, the greatest power of all was the bond I had with the **Fin-tastic Four**.

Nothing in the whole wide ocean would ever change that.